First American Edition, 1985.
Text copyright © 1985 by David Lloyd. Illustrations copyright © 1985 by
Peter Cross. All rights reserved under International and Pan-American
Copyright Conventions. Published in the United States by Random House,
Inc., New York. Published in Great Britain by Walker Books Ltd., London.

Library of Congress Cataloging in Publication Data:
Lloyd, David. Silly games. (Dinosaur days)
SUMMARY: A little dinosaur enjoys playing with his
mother.
1. Children's stories, English. [1. Dinosaurs — Fiction.
2. Prehistoric animals — Fiction. 3. Play — Fiction]
I. Cross, Peter, ill.   II. Title.   III. Series: Lloyd,
David. Dinosaur days. PZ7.L774Si 1985   [E]   84-27697
ISBN: 0-394-87380-7

Manufactured in Italy

1 2 3 4 5 6 7 8 9 0

SILLY GAMES

Written by David Lloyd
Illustrated by Peter Cross

Random House New York

Little So-and-So
was being silly.

Jumpetty

Jumpetty

JUMP

He bounced on
So-So-Slowly's tummy.

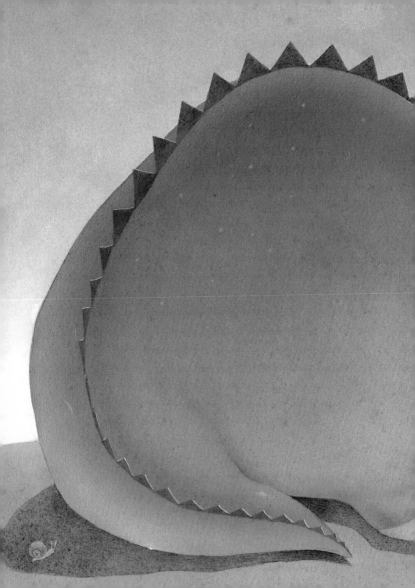

So-So-Slowly
rolled over.
Little So-and-So
danced onto her nose.

hoppity
hoppity
hop

So-So-Slowly stood up.

°°°°°°°°°°°°°°°°OOOOOO

It was a long, long way
to the ground.

So-So-Slowly strode
across the world.

Little So-and-So
raced and chased
around her feet.

ohhhhhhhhhhh

They saw Atlas,
the giant mountain turtle.

a*hhhhhhhhhhh*

They saw
little Eohippus.

They came to
the water hole.

gurgle slurp

The dinosaurs
were drinking.

So-So-Slowly sucked in
gallons of water.

shooowhh

Her cheeks were
green balloons.

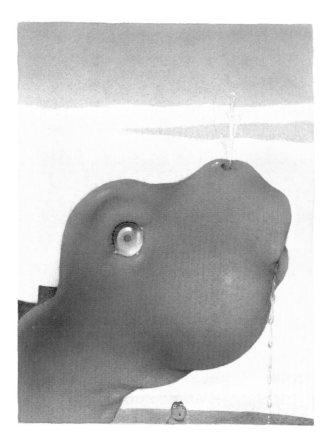

So-So-Slowly blew
out the water,
just for fun.

whooshhhhh

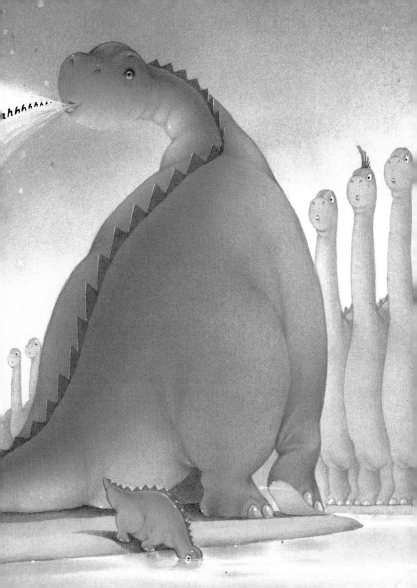

Little So-and-So
blew water
at High-and-Mighty.

phht phtt

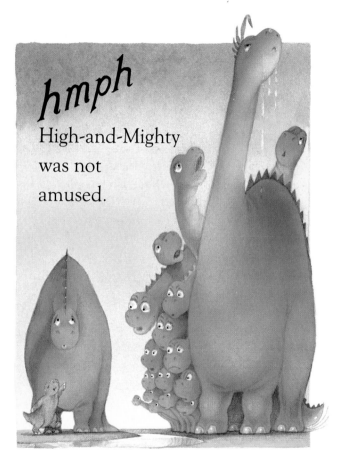

hmph

High-and-Mighty
was not
amused.

So-So-Slowly took
Little So-and-So away.

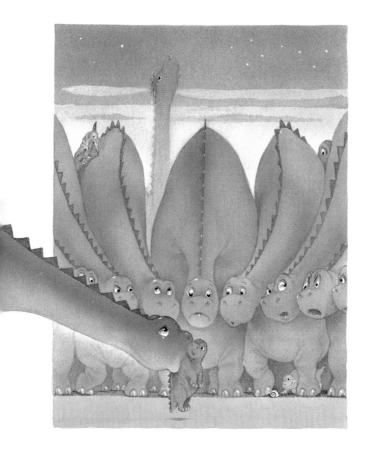

The last rays of the sun
shone softly
on the dinosaurs.

Good night, So-So-Slowly.
Good night, Little So-and-So.
It's time to sleep.